Arthur Christopher Benson

**Lord Vyet**

And other Poems

Arthur Christopher Benson

**Lord Vyet**
*And other Poems*

ISBN/EAN: 9783337401320

Printed in Europe, USA, Canada, Australia, Japan

Cover: Foto ©Andreas Hilbeck / pixelio.de

More available books at **www.hansebooks.com**

# LORD VYET

## AND

# OTHER POEMS

BY

ARTHUR CHRISTOPHER BENSON

*Of Eton College*

τελευταῖον δὲ πάντων ξυνίσταται
ἡ ἁρμονία, καὶ πρῶτον ἀπόλλυται

JOHN LANE THE BODLEY HEAD
LONDON AND NEW YORK
1897

TO

The Hon. Maurice Baring

# DEDICATION

*Friend, of my infinite dreams*
*Little enough endures;*
*Little howe'er it seems,*
*It is yours, all yours.*

*Fame hath a fleeting breath,*
*Hopes may be frail or fond;*
*But Love shall be Love till death,*
*And perhaps beyond.*

# CONTENTS

vii

# CONTENTS

## SONNETS

viii

# PRELUDE

Hushed is each busy shout :
The reverent people wait,
To see the sacred pomp stream out
Beside the temple-gate.

The bull with garlands hung,
Stern priests in vesture grim :
With rolling voices swiftly sung
Peals out the jocund hymn.

In front, behind, beside,
Beneath the chiming towers,
Pass boys that fling the censer wide,
And striplings scattering flowers.

I                    B

# PRELUDE

*Victim or minister*
*I dare not claim to be,*
*But in the concourse and the stir,*
*There shall be room for me.*

*The victim feels the stroke:*
*The priests are bowed in prayer :—*
*I feed the porch with fragrant smoke,*
*Strew roses on the stair.*

# LORD VYET

WHAT, must my lord be gone ?
  Command his horse, and call
  The servants, one and all.
" Nay, nay, I go alone."

My Lord, I shall unfold
  Thy cloak of sables rare
  To shield thee from the air :
" Nay, nay, I must be cold."

At least thy leech I'll tell
  Some drowsy draught to make,
  Less thou should toss awake.
" Nay, nay, I shall sleep well."

My lady keeps her bower :—
I hear the lute delight
The dark and frozen night,
High up within the tower.

Wilt thou that she descend?
Thy son is in the hall,
Tossing his golden ball,
Shall he my lord attend?

" Nay, sirs, unbar the door,
The broken lute shall fall;
My son will leave his ball
To tarnish on the floor."

Yon bell to triumph rings!
To greet thee, monarchs wait
Beside their palace gate.
" Yes, I shall sleep with kings,"

4

My lord will soon alight
   With some rich prince, his friend,
   Who shall his ease attend.
" I shall lodge low to-night."

My lord hath lodging nigh?
   " Yes, yes, I go not far,—
   And yet the furthest star
Is not so far as I."

# THE SIREN

Rest thee in a field of fountains:
　　Wanderer, wilt thou further go?
Range the large and lonely mountains?
　　"Ah, no, no!"

Here the welling wave shall strengthen
　　Thee, to brave the further stress;
Rest thee, till the shadows lengthen:—
　　"Ah, yes, yes!"

See, the angry sun grows stronger,
　　Faintly smiles the weary day;
Wanderer, rest a little longer;
　　Ah, stay, stay!

6

See, the place of storms, the hated
  Ridge, with high and hungry crest:
Thou art even now belated:
    So rest, rest!

" Nay, alas! I fear to lose me
  In the hot land's drowsy breath:
But a dreadful voice pursues me
    Saying ' Death, Death,'

" Through the wide and wintry heaven,
  To the aching vales of frost,
Where the wind shall wail at even,
    Crying ' Lost, Lost.' "

# A TRIO

I, and the Bird,
  And the Wind together,
Sang a supplication
  In the winter weather.

The Bird sang for sunshine,
  And trees of winter fruit,
And love in the spring-time,
  When the thickets shoot.

And I sang for patience
  When the teardrops start:
Clean hands and clear eyes,
  And a faithful heart.

## A TRIO

And the Wind thereunder,
As we faintly cried,
Breathed a bass of wonder,
Blowing deep and wide.

# THE RAILWAY

Upon the iron highway, wreathed in smoke,
  Or East or West the clanking engine reels,
The weary dust spins onward at the stroke
    Of half-a-hundred wheels.

It comes, the breathless driver staring straight
  Through misty eye-holes, with the sudden
    gleam
Of burnished dome, and cranks of ponderous
    weight,
    And clouds of hissing steam.

Old countrymen, that trudge from new-ploughed
    lands,

And on high bridges stay their weary feet,
See faces flashed beneath them, waving hands
That may not stay to greet.

Or slow, with hollow blast and wealthy din,
By wide-armed signals creeps the laden train,
High vans with shuddering jolt, and clinking pin,
And hiss of clattering chain.

Wide-eyed, affrighted cattle, meek and still :
And murky coal for city folk to burn,
And dusty blocks hewed from some Western hill,
And wreathed in twisted fern.

But best of all, when, in the sullen night,
Along the dim embankment, hung in air,
Shoots the red streamer, linked with cheerful light;
The wide-flung furnace-glare

Lights the dim hedges and the rolling steam:—
 Then passes, and in narrowing distance dies,
Tracked by the watchful lanterns' lessening
    gleam—
    Two red resentful eyes.

And some are borne to dim and alien shores,
 And some return to merriment and home:—
These, while the train through slumbering
    homestead roars
    Thrill with delight:—and some

Fly from the horror that their hands have
    wrought,
 And shudder, as the shivering engine reels;
They fly, but falter: one red-throated thought
    Pants ever at their heels.

# THE MOWER

WHET thy scythe, mower,
  Though thy hand swing slow,
The sun falls lower,
  And the shadows grow.

How the white blade flashes
  In the steady sun !
All the dinted slashes
  Tell the death of one.

Field-flower and clover,
  Sword-grass seeded high,
Summer dreams are over,
  Side by side they lie.

13

# THE MOWER

Winds above them lying
  Stir with fragrant feet;
Who would shrink from dying
  If death smelt so sweet?

From the sturdy shoulder
  Let the scythe be swung;
Soon the blade shall moulder,
  In the granary hung.

Iron steeds of battle
  Snort o'er humming farms:
Hear them clink and rattle,
  Lifting solemn arms!

Whet thy scythe bolder,
  Evening comes apace:
One with scythe on shoulder
  Runs a rival race.

Through the whispering grasses
   Let the bright blade ring;
Ere the good time passes,
   Mower, stride and swing.

# LIVE-BAIT

THE weir was fragrant, with the scent
   Of falling streams and trailing weeds;
The careful angler leaned intent,
   And cast his net beyond the reeds:
Three silvery dace imprisoned there
Were dragged all gasping to the air.

One from the dripping net he took,
   And squeezed his tender body hard,
And pierced him with his cruel hook
   That all his limber mouth was marred:
Then cast him where the stream gushed out
To be a bait for Master Trout.

So all that golden afternoon
  He strove and swam—now dangled high,
Now plunged afresh :. and oh, so soon
  As he hath gained his liberty,
Must swing and flicker, sorely spent
Within the dazzling firmament.

At evensong he sobbed and died.
  I know not! but did God forget
That day upon the water side ?
  Or cast him sternly in the net ?
Oh broken dreams, oh cruel lot!
Would I could think that God forgot!

# THE SHEPHERD

THE shepherd is an ancient man,
   His back is bent, his foot is slow;
Although the heavens he doth not scan,
      He scents what winds shall blow.

His face is like the pippin, grown
   Red ripe, in frosty suns that shone;
'Tis hard and wrinkled, as a stone
      The rains have rained upon.

When tempests sweep the dripping plain,
   He stands unmoved beneath the hedge,
And sees the columns of the rain,
      The storm-cloud's shattered edge.

18

When frosts among the misty farms
　　Make crisp the surface of the loam,
He shivering claps his creaking arms,
　　But would not sit at home.

Short speech he hath for man and beast ;
　　Some fifty words are all his store.
Why should his language be increased ?
　　He hath no need for more.

There is no change he doth desire,
　　Of far-off lands he hath not heard ;
Beside his wife, before the fire,
　　He sits, and speaks no word.

He holds no converse with his kind,
　　On birds and beasts his mind is bent ;
He knows the thoughts that stir their mind,
　　Love, hunger, hate, content.

# THE SHEPHERD

Of kings and wars he doth not hear.
   He tells the seasons that have been
By stricken oaks and hunted deer,
     And strange fowl he has seen.

In Church, some muttering he doth make,
   Well-pleased when hymns harmonious rise;
He doth not strive to overtake
     The hurrying litanies.

He hears the music of the wind,
   His prayer is brief, and scant his creed;
The shadow, and what lurks behind,
     He doth not greatly heed.

# ONE BY ONE

One by one, as evening closes,
  Droop the flowers that drank the sun;
See, they sleep, my weary roses,
    One by one:

Never did I bend above you,
  O my flowers, while all was bright;
There is time, I said, to love you
    Ere the night.

You were neither watched nor tended,
  Fevered thoughts were mine instead,
Now the weary day is ended;—
    You are dead.

# ONE BY ONE

Now I come in dumb disorder,
 Seek and search, in wild regret,
If one rose in bed or border
 Wakens yet.

Nay, they slumber till the morrow!
 Hasten homewards : bar the gate.
Through the cold dark hours of sorrow
 I will wait.

# WHEN PUNCTUAL DAWN

When punctual dawn came o'er the hill,
In orange veiled and tender blue,
Wan in the dark field gleamed the rill,
The dusky hedge was gemmed with dew.

And patient sheep from folded feet
Rose one by one, alert for food,
And one by one, so small and sweet,
The flattened grass-stems stirred and stood.

And I too rose, and stepping down
Drank deep the invigorating air,
And scanned the little sleeping town,
And thanked my God that I was there.

# "THE EARTH HATH DRUNK DEEP"

THE earth hath drunk deep
Of the rains of God :
When men were asleep.
On the thirsty sod,
On the dusty town,
Most silent and steep
Did the rain leap down.

And the delicate stems
Of the grass are clean,
And the elders are green,
And the rose is brimmed with gems.

24

## "THE EARTH HATH DRUNK DEEP"

My heart hath drunk deep
Of the wine of God :
When men were asleep
Were the dark grapes trode,
And the acrid must—
Oh ! the draught was deep—
To my lips was thrust :—

Shadows and fears
Were the bitter part
Of the craven heart,
And the cup was brimmed with tears.

# IN ETON CHURCHYARD

In and out I tread the slender
   Paths that wind by grave and grave;
In the summer breeze the tender
   Grasses wave.

Jackdaws cheerily hallooing
   From the turret's dizzy edge:
Glossy doves serenely cooing
   From their ledge.

Through the stillness, faint and dreamy,
   Comes the murmur of the town,
Where the thorn tree shakes her creamy
   Petals down.

Brothers, sisters, silent lying,
　　Ere you breathed the last long breath,
Were you too afraid of dying,
　　Not of death ?

Do you walk unseen beside us ?
　　Prompt, applaud our dreams of good ?
Would you comfort, warn us, guide us,
　　If you could ?

Children, tired of idle jesting,
　　Locked in dear embraces weep :
Sink reluctant, sink protesting
　　Into sleep.

Tho' the host that none can number
　　Greet upon the joyful shore,
I should be content to slumber
　　Evermore.

# THE ARTIST IN CHURCH

Lord Christ, hast Thou no word for me,
   Thou high and humble soul?
Thine ailing creatures turn to Thee
From their abiding misery,
   And wonder, and are whole.

Strong words Thou hast for knave and king,
   For publican and priest,
For flowers that bloom, and birds that sing,
For every small or suffering thing,
   Sad man and patient beast:

For us with our awakened eyes,
   With skilled and careful hands,

28

Who harvest from the sunset skies
A sense of gracious mysteries,
  Thou hast no dear commands ?

Hath Thomas faith, hath Peter zeal,
  Hath Paul his words of fire ?
Not less imperiously I feel,
Not less insistently I kneel
  Before my pure desire.

Ay, I can preach Thee, I can trace,
  With firm and strenuous line,
The awful splendours of the Face,
The shrouded effluence of the grace
  Too urgently Divine.

Lo in our eyes the tear-drops start,
  We swim in stormy seas :
Hast Thou within Thine ample heart,

No shelter for the sons of art,
   No room for such as these ?

Or wert Thou silent of design,
   Because Thy thought was cold ?
Doth love of word, of hue, of line,
Sequester from Thy power divine,
   Dissociate from Thy fold ?

O words of Power, O gracious deeds !
   When Thou didst dwell with men,
Thou didst divine their deepest needs :
I marvel, and my spirit bleeds
   That Thou wast silent then.

# MY OLD FRIEND

IT seems the world was always bright
  With some divine unclouded weather,
When we, with hearts and footsteps light,
  By lawn and river walked together:

There was no talk of me and you,
  Of theories with facts to bound them,
We were content to be and do,
  And take our fortunes as we found them.

We spoke no wistful words of love,
  No hint of sympathy and dearness,
Only around, beneath, above,
  There ran a swift and subtle nearness.

# MY OLD FRIEND

Each inmost thought was known to each
    By some impetuous divination :
We found no need of flattering speech,
    Content with silent admiration.

I think I never touched your hand,
    I took no heed of face or feature,
Only, I thought, on sea or land
    Was never such a gracious creature.

It seems I was not hard to please,
    Where'er you led I needs must follow;
For strength you were my Hercules,
    For wit and lustre my Apollo.

The years flew onward : stroke by stroke
    They clashed from the impartial steeple,
And we appear to other folk
    A pair of ordinary people.

One word, old friend : though fortune flies,
 If hope should fail—till death shall sever—
In one dim pair of faithful eyes
 You seem as bright, as brave as ever.

# THE OWL

WHEN the winds overhead were sweeping,
    And the whole loud woodland was astir,
You were perched, like a weary hermit, sleeping
    In a dark tangled fork of the fir.

But at last when the tired wind was winging
    To the edge of the smouldering light,
Your laughter, wild and horrible, came ringing
    And sent a sudden chill through the night.

You laughed, demoniacally dreaming
    Of the rush of the startled mouse,
When you with your grey wing gleaming
    Sweep low o'er his heathery house.

And quiet woodland things without number,

   Who were couched in bracken and in brake,

Shivered chill, on the edge of slumber,

   At the thought of a wicked thing awake.


Thrice you turned your hornèd head in the
     shadow,

   And blinked with impenetrable eyes,

Then out over copse and misty meadow

   You swept under shrouded skies.


The bell beat one in the village,

   With the firelight red in the room,

As you came and went, to slay and to pillage,

   With your soft wing flapping in the gloom.

# THE RINGDOVE

Grey dove, that croonest in the solemn fir,
    Lost in unutterable, deep content,
Soon will the drowsy forest be astir,
    Soon will the loud wind thunder imminent.
But while the shadows lengthen, while the light
    Slants from the West across the red-stemmed
        grove,
Croon thy soft lay of intimate delight,
    Of rapturous solitude, and gracious love.

Thou from the branching fastness canst discern
    The woodways winding green, the island knolls
Crowned with tall oaks, and rimmed with rusty
    fern,

The beeches, with their plain and rounded
  boles,
Widespreading, over smooth and crackling floors;
  The chestnuts splashed with golden bravery,
The pine, a slender pyramid, that soars
  With velvet greenness to the freer sky.

Croon as thou wilt: no enemy is near:
  Close for awhile thy proud and wary eyes,
Speak to my heart, while yet I linger near,
  Thy patient peace, thy languorous mysteries.
Left to herself, how musical of mood
  The world's old heart, beside her chosen
    shore!
The din, the shattering tumult, and the rude
  Thunder of battle should be heard no more.

No more the wild uproarious thirst of life,
  The din of words whose purpose is the same:

# THE RINGDOVE

The weary enmities, the feverous strife,
  Here in this peace are nothing but a name.
Peace, strenuous peace, is thine and mine to-day,
  Sedatest energy, divine desire,
This be my part in thy unconscious lay,—
  Strongly to hope and softly to aspire.

# THE CAT

On some grave business, soft and slow
Along the garden-paths you go,
  With bold and burning eyes:
Or stand, with twitching tail, to mark
What starts and rustles in the dark,
  Among the peonies.

The dusty cockchafer that springs
Upon the dusk with whirring wings,
  The beetle glossy-horned,
The rabbit pattering through the fern,
May frisk unheeded, by your stern
  Preoccupation scorned.

You go, and when the morning dawns
O'er blowing trees and dewy lawns,

39

# THE CAT

Dim-veiled with gossamer,
When cheery birds are on the wing,
You creep, a wild and wicked thing,
With stained and starting fur.

You all day long, beside the fire,
Retrace in dreams your dark desire,
And mournfully complain,
In grave displeasure, if I raise
Your languid form to pet or praise;—
And so to sleep again.

The gentler hound, that near me lies,
Looks up with true and tender eyes,
And waits my generous mirth;
You do not woo me, but demand
A gift from my unwilling hand,
A tribute to your worth.

# THE CAT

You loved me when the fire was warm,
But now I stretch a fondling arm,
   You eye me and depart.
Cold eyes, sleek skin, and velvet paws,
You win my indolent applause,
   You do not win my heart.

# THE HAWK

The hawk slipt out of the pine, and rose in the
sunlit air:

Steady and still he poised; his shadow slept on
the grass:

And the bird's song sickened and sank: she
cowered with furtive stare

Dumb, till the quivering dimness should flicker
and shift and pass.

Suddenly down he dropped: she heard the hiss
of his wing,

Fled with a scream of terror: oh, would she
had dared to rest!

For the hawk at eve was full, and there was no
bird to sing,

And over the heather drifted the down from a
bleeding breast.

# THE BARBEL

Bearded Barbel, swimming deep
  In the cool translucent gloom,
Poised in contemplative sleep,
  In your liquid moving room :

Where the watery gleams transfuse
  Coated rush and sleek strong reed,
Up the swaying avenues,
  Rimmed with plumed and velvet weed :

Bearded Barbel, you survey
  Hour by hour the pebbly floor :
Have you ne'er a wish to stray
  Wider from the willowy shore ?

43

Have you ne'er a wilful wonder
    Whence the dancing bubbles gleam,
Whence the broad weir's drowsy thunder
    Mutters down the murmuring stream ?

Bearded Barbel, be content !
    Your dim world is small and sweet ;
Let your safer merriment
    Laugh to scorn our restless feet.

If your curious wilful greed
    Tempt you, ah the illusive gleam !
You will suffer, you will bleed,
    Writhing in the troubled stream.

Sweeps a wild bewildering glare :
    Gleams your silver mail beneath :
Then the thin and acid air
    Chokes your faint and sobbing breath.

# THE WISHING WELL

Yes, here's the place : the meadow thick with
   rushes,
The gravelly hill, the elms beside the pool,
Here through the dancing sand it jets and gushes,
   Divinely clear and cool.

Now must I kneel and set my palms together,—
   So runs the rite,—and then, devoutly bowed,
Face down the wind, so it be windy weather,
   Then speak my wish aloud.

No vague desires, virtue and health combining,
   Not love—but one inevitable name,
Not wealth, but cash—describing and defining
   The very coin I claim.

45

Then O bright hope, with no success to dim it,

Vast vague desires, of you I dare not think !

Dear boundless dreams I must curtail and limit !

Nay, nay ! I will not drink.

# JACK IN THE BOX

THE bolt is slipped, the wiry rings
    Release their struggling mystery:
The merry monster, out he springs,
    With whiskered cheek and cheery eye!
He leaps and claps his cymballed hands,
Then still in frozen silence stands.

Come, cram the ruddy rascal down,
    Thrust pointed chin on springy breast:
No matter, let him fret and frown,
    Within his cedarn prison prest:
Through hours of anguish let him gain
New strength to spring and clap again.

When Epimetheus half undid
    Pandora's box in surly greed,

Slipping from out the lifted lid,
   Came darling dream, and pretty deed,
And fifty sweet imaginings
With beaded eyes and filmy wings.

" For shame, for shame," Prometheus cried,
   " Dear silly brother, they are sped :—
Nay throw the vacant casket wide,
   It prisons one ethereal head :
Still nestling in the fragrant dusk
Lies hope, a frail and faded husk."

Spring up, and clap thy nimble hands,
   O irrepressible delight !
At thy light-hearted shrill demands
   Our burdened hearts grow strong and bright :
Though faith wax faint and love take wing,
Unreasoning hope shall leap and sing.

# THE PHŒNIX

By feathers green, across Casbeen,
  The pilgrims track the Phœnix flown,
By gems he strewed in waste and wood,
  And jewelled plumes at random thrown.

Till wandering far, by moon and star,
  They stand beside the fruitful pyre,
Whence breaking bright with sanguine light,
  The impulsive bird forgets his sire.

Those ashes shine like ruby wine,
  Like bag of Tyrian murex spilt,
The claw, the jowl of the flying fowl
  Are with the glorious anguish gilt.

# THE PHŒNIX

So rare the light, so rich the sight,
 Those pilgrim men, on profit bent,
Drop hands and eyes and merchandise,
 And are with gazing most content.

# EVENSONG

THRUSH, sing clear, for the spring is here :
Sing, for the summer is near, is near,

All day long thou hast plied thy song,
Hardly hid from the hurrying throng:

Now the shade of the trees is laid
Down the meadow and up the glade:

Now when the air grows cool and rare
Birds of the cloister fall to prayer:

Here is the bed of the patient dead,
Shoulder by shoulder, head by head.

Sweet bells swing in the tower, and ring
Men to worship before their King.

# EVENSONG

See they come as the grave bells hum,
Restless voices awhile are dumb:

More and more on the sacred floor
Feet that linger about the door:

Sweet sounds swim through the vaulting dim,
Psalm and canticle, vesper hymn.

That is the way that mortals pray:
Which is the sweeter? brown bird, say!

Which were best for me? both are blest;
Sing thy sweetest and leave the rest.

# SELF

THIS is my chiefest torment, that behind
   This brave and subtle spirit, this swift brain,
   There sits and shivers, in a cell of pain,
A central atom, melancholy, blind,

Which is myself: tho' when spring suns are kind,
   And rich leaves riot in the genial rain,
   I cheat him dreaming, slip my rigorous chain,
Free as a skiff before the dancing wind.

Then he awakes, and vexed that I am glad,
   In dreary malice strains some nimble chord,
     Pricks his thin claw within some tingling
     nerve:
   And all at once I falter, start, and swerve
From my true course, and fall, unmanned and sad,
   Into gross darkness, tangible, abhorred.

Yet I can send my thought from sun to sun,
Behind the stars, beyond the eternal night;
Pierce through the whirling spheres of fervent
light,
Or nearer roam: hither and thither run;

Strain to a sharp and icy summit, thread
The poisonous depth of some hot forest maze,
Or haunt the dark sea-bottom's glimmering
ways,
Where sunken wrecks hang silent overhead.

Now, in a sun-dried city of the south,
Linger through dusty vineyards, branching
palms;—
The shrill cicalas chirping in the drouth;—
Or swim by coral islets, floating free
And eager, parting with imagined arms
The crystal rollers of a sapphire sea.

Or I constrain the poets to my call;—
    With Homer, staff in hand, and lyre on back,
    Stumbling and sightless on the upland track,
Or praised and honoured in the echoing hall,

Hear from his lips the rolling thunders fall;
    Or sit with Virgil in the orchard-edge,
    Hearing the bees hum in the privet hedge,
And deep-mouthed cattle lowing from the stall.

Or I can follow Una's peerless knight
    Riding alone in mountain solitudes,
        Where Awbey leaps from Bally-howra hill;
        Or trace the clear impetuous Rotha rill,
    With Wordsworth, mouthing music in the
        woods,
His eyes transfigured with a sacred light.

Or I can trace the cycles that have been,
　　See silent priests, dead Cæsars, face to face;
　　Laugh with old wits, with serious statesmen
　　　　pace,
Peep unobserved at many a secret scene.

Thence through wild woods my dreaming way
　　　　I take,
　　Through ancient cities piled of ponderous
　　　　stones,
　　Or dripping caverns carpeted with bones,
To wattled huts isled in a mountain lake.

Backwards, still backwards, till the glowing earth
　　Lose beast and tree, and show her haggard scars;
To chaos, and the chill sun's nebulous birth:—
　　Above, beneath, the flaming æons roll:—
　　Still in its cold cell sits the brooding soul,
More to itself than thirty thousand stars.

# KEATS

LAUGHING thou said'st, 'Twere hell for thee to
   fail

   In thy vast purpose, in thy brave design,

   Ere thy young cheek, with passion's venomed
   wine

Flushed and grew pale, ah me! flushed and grew
   pale !

Where is thy music now ?   In hearts that pine

   O'erburdened, for the clamorous world too frail,

   Yet love the charméd dusk, the nightingale,

Not for her sweet sake only, but for thine.

Thy name is writ in water, ay, 'tis writ

   As when the moon, a chill and friendless thing,

      Passes and writes her will upon the tide,

   And piles the ocean in a moving ring :

And every stagnant bay is brimmed with it,

      Each mast-fringed port, each estuary wide.

# VICTORY

So, I have gained a crown and lost a friend.
  What, was he envious of my climbing fame,
  Did he aspire to what I did not claim,
Mistake the summit that I dared ascend?
And I, who chiefly toiled that I might spend
  My hoarded hopes to crown his tardier name,
  Sad and alone, in solitude and shame,
Sit mourning, careless what the fates may send.

So David, when the fiercest fight was won,
  Recked not of all the faithful hearts that bled
    To comfort him, to guard his troubled days:
    He to his Captains spoke no word of praise,
  But wailed in cold unreasoning grief, and said:
" O my son Absalom, my son, my son."

# THE PURSUIT

I HAD outstripped him on the moorland wide,
   The heathery moor, with grassy tracks between
   The peaty hills : at eve he should have been
A moving speck upon the far hill-side.

But here within the tangled forest, here
   With all these trailing vines about my feet,
   Among the tall tree-stems, he steps as fleet
As I, though I be winged with instant fear.

For every clutching branch I rend away,
   Each knotted creeper, tremblingly untied,
     Each hazel thicket, where I bend and crawl,
   Leaves free the perilous gap for him to glide
     Still nearer, till with sobbing breath I fall
Upon my face, and he shall spring and slay.

# THE GENTIAN

SAY gentian, by what daring alchemy
  Dost thou distil from cold and weary stones,
  From tumbled rocks, the spent earth's staring
    bones,
The intensest essence of the unclouded sky?

Is it through dreaming, night by weary night,
  Through still pale months beneath the drifted
    snow,
  Dreaming of sunshine and warm fields aglow,
Of azure depths, vast leagues of tranquil light?

Not thine the outrageous splendours of the morn,
  The crimson pomp of sunset, the brisk ray
Of the heavenly arch, of watery conflict born,
    But the pure radiance of the untroubled
      heaven
    When the eye dives, in headlong rapture
      driven,
  Zone beyond zone, and finds no stop nor stay.

# THE GRASSHOPPER

REST, rest, impatient heart, thou dost not know
  What 'tis thou seekest: wilt thou hurl away
For petty praise, a little gilded show,
  The lavish treasure of the golden day?

Yon grasshopper, in green enamelled mail,
  With waving whisks and blunted nose upthrust,
Draws whizzing thighs athwart his plated tail,
  Or trails his belly in the sun-warmed dust,

Or leaps among his fellows, caring nought
  Which leaps the highest, which the braver drest;
  With solemn face his edged jaws crossing slow
He clips the succulent salad: gives no thought
  That soon the clouds shall gather from the West,
  And all the high hill-pastures ache with snow.

# UTTERANCE

I HAVE strung my harp, and tuned each subtle chord
   To truest consonance, and day by day
   Have trained my tripping fingers how to stray
With swift unerring motions.  I have stored

My mind with every grave melodious tone,
   Each eager modulation, deftly planned
   O'er perilous gaps to reach a welcoming hand:—
Yet cannot frame a music of my own.

O for that hour when, with reverberant wings,
   Some airy thought, deliberate, at my call,
     Shall drop beside me, whispering in my ear :
     And I shall seize my harp, and thrill to hear
   The pent-up music ripple and break, with all
My heart's rich secrets echoing down the strings.

# ANNIVERSARIES

When I was yet a child, my sparkling days
   Spake little with each other, but with joy
   Each sprang to life, by favourite friend or toy
Distinguished, walking in familiar ways ;

Each in itself a breathing mystery,
   Portending nought, save through the lagging
      weeks,
   In restless foot, in flushed and eager cheeks,
Savour and sound of the imagined sea.

But now they talk together, and are sad ;—
   " To-day," they say, " how short a time ago,
     We laid her, weeping, in the churchyard
      ground: "
     And one saith, " ere the solemn year move
      round,
Shall this be reft from me that makes me glad? "
     And all make answer, saying " Even so."

# THE LONG SLEEP

As one that wakes and from his pillow leaps,
  With some fierce dream, some visionary shock,
  Or gusty chiding of the turret-clock,
And deems it time for labour, till he creeps

Dumb and bewildered, to the window-bars,
  And sees the pale lamp on the roadway shed
  Strange wafts of shifting shade, and overhead
Troop through the black night the slow-marching
    stars:

Then is he glad at heart, and knows the day
  Is yet far off, and trims the smouldering fire,
And with delicious tremors, doth allay
    His languorous head, and dives to slumber
    deep;—
  Even with such eager longing, I desire
  Death, and the dumb interminable sleep.

# THE MESSAGE

STRETCHED in the grass, what was it that I
    dreamed?
  There, where the mossy rock its streamlet
    spilled,
  While the sad curlew in the rushes trilled,
And flying sails by distant headlands gleamed;

Hot o'er the heather waved the quivering air,
  Sweep after sweep the billowy moorland rolled,
  As tho' some stiff green coverlet did enfold
Huge sleeping giants, sprawling prostrate there.

What was it that I dreamed? the soaring bird
  Swept wold and waste, yet saw not what I saw:
  Not love, not honour, not the perfect mind!
But how to tell the secret that I heard
  Sung by the stream, and whispered in the wind,
Of faith and patience, and divinest awe?

# REST

TO-DAY I'll give to peace; I will not look
  Behind, before me; I will simply be;
  Hopes and regrets shall claim no share in me;
Here I will lie beside the limpid brook,
And turn the pages of some aimless book,
  Sunk and submerged in vague felicity;
  Live, mute and still, in what I feel and see,
The dreaming guardian of the upland nook.

Well! here's my world to-day! cicalas spare
  Sawing harsh music; beetles big, that grope
    Among the grass-stems; merry flies astir;
And goats with impudent face and silken hair,
  That poise and tinkle on the Western slope,
  Breast-deep in Alpen-rose and juniper.

# THE POET

HE shall be great, and something more than great,
  But human first: and nought of human known
  Shall slip unnoted from his meshes, thrown
With wary hand in secret seas of fate.

So great, so human, that the song he sings
  Seems but the faint effulgence of the soul,
  That dived to hell, and rising, pure and whole,
Beat in the sunlit air her happy wings.

His soul shall be a valley full of trees ;
  Pines for soft sound, and limes for scent and
    shade,
    Where birds may nest, blithe thrush and
      bright-eyed wren,
  Flowers for delight, and fruit for healing made,
    And heart of oak, to build the homes of men,
And swim secure in thunder-throated seas.

# O LACRIMARUM FONS

O HOLIEST fount of sorrow, treasured tears;
  O eager consolation of sick grief;
  That bring to burdened sadness pure relief,
Ye have no fellowship with craven fears!

True tears are sorrow's guerdon, for they prove
  The worth of suffering, that the sacred dart
  Hath struck, and shivered the incredulous heart,
And pierced the secret amplitude of love.

For of thy shafts, that hourly past us flame,
  Some taint and mar our innocence, and some
    Are bent and blunted by the stubborn mind,
Or throb and rankle in the tortured frame:
    But I will pray, if Thy strong hands are
      kind,
  "Let them strike home, my God, let them
    strike home."

# INDOLENCE

WHAT, hath the dark surprised me as I dreamed?
  The hours were mine: I neither swooned nor
    slept,
  Only the slow shade o'er the dial crept,
And peace was thrice as peaceful as it seemed.

Ah me! I have not earned the right to sleep,
  Nor strung my thews for battle: I have spent
  The hoarded coin that was for increase lent,
Dreamed of the harvest that I may not reap.

Waste, trivial waste! fickle and fruitless moods,
  Dear to the mind of God! Shall nature then
    Bewail the helpless debt she cannot pay?
  Petals that bloom, and fall, unseen of men:
Slow springs that drip in mountain solitudes,
  Rocks that the sad sea sprinkles twice a day.

69

# PRID. KAL. OCT.

O Asian birds, that round me in the gloom
 Patter and peck unseen, or with loud stroke
 Soar to the covert of some branching oak,—
To-morrow comes the destined hecatomb.

Shout once again your strident orisons,
 Thanks for the dewy morning, for the food
 By hands unseen at woodland corners strewed,
For water cool, that through the thicket runs.

To-morrow comes the end:—the wood astir
 With patient tramping figures, and the noise
 Of tree-trunks tapped, the cry of eager boys,
 The startled rush, and battling as you rise
Above the copse, beyond the topmost fir,
 Death, lightning death, amid the echoing
 skies.

# DEATH

THE soul, that dizzied with the din of death,
  The roar of clamorous blood in failing ears,
  Still sees the sickly swimming day, and hears
The rattling in-take of his sobbing breath:

Then cleaves the dark slow, tranquillising tide,
  And swims in silent waters, careless now
  If still they press his hand, and kiss his brow,
But snaps the parting strands, and wanders wide,—

Then, in one glowing instant, that atones
  For woe and fear, made one with life and light,
    He watches, as he hangs in wondering ease,
    Poised in the dusk, the red earth with her seas
And islands, snowy poles and sunlit zones,
  Thunder and heave, and leap across the night.

# ENVOI

I cannot sing as sings the nightingale
 Frenzied with rapture, big with rich delight,
Till lovers lean together, passion-pale,
 And chide the awestruck silence of the night.

I cannot sing as sings the tranquil thrush,
 O'er dewy thicket and untrodden lawn,
When early gossamers veil the frosted bush,
 In the chaste freshness of the sparkling dawn.

I cannot sing as sings the brooding dove,
 At windless noon, in her high towers of green,
A song of deep content, untroubled love,
 With many a meditative pause between.

72

# ENVOI

*I cannot sing, as sings the dauntless owl*
  *His shout of horror at a dark dead hour :*
*When the hair pricks, and startled watch-dogs*
    *howl,*
  *And night-bells clamour in the lonely tower.*

*But I can sing as sings the prudent bee,*
  *As hour by patient hour he goes and comes,*
*Bearing the golden dust from tree to tree,*
  *Labours in hope, and as he labours, hums.*

Printed by R. Folkard & Son,
22, Devonshire St., Queen Sq., London.

# JOHN LANE

THE
BODLEY
HEAD
VIGO ST
W.
*Telegrams*
"BODLEIAN
LONDON"

CATALOGUE *of* PUBLICATIONS
*in* BELLES LETTRES *all at net prices*

# List of Books

IN

## *BELLES LETTRES*

# Published by John Lane

### ᴄ𝔥e 𝔅oδℓeᵖ 𝔥eaδ

VIGO STREET, LONDON, W.

**Adams (Francis).**
ESSAYS IN MODERNITY. Crown 8vo.
5s. net. [*Shortly.*
A CHILD OF THE AGE. (*See* KEY-
NOTES SERIES.)

**A. E.**
HOMEWARD SONGS BY THE WAY.
Sq. 16mo, wrappers. 1s. 6d. net.
*Transferred to the present Pub-*
*lisher.* [*Second Edition.*

**Aldrich (T. B.)**
LATER LYRICS. Sm. Fcap. 8vo.
2s. 6d. net.

**Allen (Grant).**
THE LOWER SLOPES : A Volume of
Verse. With Title-page and Cover
Design by J. ILLINGWORTH KAY.
Crown 8vo. 5s. net.
THE WOMAN WHO DID. (*See* KEY-
NOTES SERIES.)
THE BRITISH BARBARIANS. (*See*
KEYNOTES SERIES.)

**Arcady Library (The).**
A Series of Open-Air Books. Edited
by J. S. FLETCHER. With Cover
Designs by PATTEN WILSON.
Each volume crown 8vo. 5s. net.
   I. ROUND ABOUT A BRIGHTON
     COACH OFFICE. By MAUDE
     EGERTON KING. With
     over 30 Illustrations by
     LUCY KEMP-WELCH.
   II. LIFE IN ARCADIA. By J. S.
     FLETCHER. Illustrated by
     PATTEN WILSON.

**Arcady Library (The)**—*cont.*
   III. SCHOLAR GIPSIES. By JOHN
     BUCHAN. With 7 full-page
     Etchings by D.Y. CAMERON
*The following is in preparation :*
   IV. IN THE GARDEN OF PEACE.
     By HELEN MILMAN. With
     Illustrations by EDMUND
     H. NEW.

**Beeching (Rev. H. C.).**
IN A GARDEN : Poems. With Title-
page designed by ROGER FRY.
Crown 8vo. 5s. net.
ST. AUGUSTINE AT OSTIA. Crown
8vo, wrappers. 1s. net.

**Beerbohm (Max).**
THE WORKS OF MAX BEERBOHM.
With a Bibliography by JOHN
LANE. Sq. 16mo. 4s. 6d. net.

**Benson (Arthur Christopher)**
LYRICS. Fcap. 8vo, buckram. 5s.
net.
LORD VYET AND OTHER POEMS.
Fcap. 8vo. 3s. 6d. net.

**Bodley Head Anthologies
(The).**
Edited by ROBERT H. CASE. With
Title-page and Cover Designs by
WALTER WEST. Each volume
crown 8vo. 5s. net.
   I. ENGLISH EPITHALAMIES.
     By ROBERT H. CASE.

## Bodley Head Anthologies (The)—continued.

II. MUSA PISCATRIX. By JOHN BUCHAN. With 6 Etchings by E. PHILIP PIMLOTT.

III. ENGLISH ELEGIES. By JOHN C BAILEY.

IV. ENGLISH SATIRES. By CHAS. HILL DICK.

## Bridges (Robert).

SUPPRESSED CHAPTERS AND OTHER BOOKISHNESS. Crown 8vo. 3s. 6d. net. [Second Edition.

## Brotherton (Mary).

ROSEMARY FOR REMEMBRANCE. With Title-page and Cover Design by WALTER WEST. Fcap. 8vo. 3s. 6d. net.

## Crackanthorpe (Hubert).

VIGNETTES. A Miniature Journal of Whim and Sentiment. Fcap. 8vo, boards. 2s. 6d. net.

## Crane (Walter).

TOY BOOKS. Re-issue, each with new Cover Design and End Papers. This LITTLE PIG'S PICTURE BOOK, containing:

I. THIS LITTLE PIG.

II. THE FAIRY SHIP.

III. KING LUCKIEBOY'S PARTY.

The three bound in one volume with a decorative cloth cover, end papers, and a newly written and designed preface and title-page. 3s. 6d. net; separately 9d. net each.

MOTHER HUBBARD'S PICTURE BOOK, containing:

I. MOTHER HUBBARD'S.

II. THE THREE BEARS.

III. THE ABSURD A. B. C.

The three bound in one volume with a decorative cloth cover, end papers, and a newly written and designed preface and title-page. 3s. 6d. net; separately 9d. net each.

## Custance (Olive).

FIRST FRUITS : Poems. Fcap. 8vo. 3s. 6d. net.

## Dalmon (C. W.).

SONG FAVOURS. With a Title-page by J. P. DONNE. Sq. 16mo. 3s. 6d. net.

## Davidson (John).

PLAYS : An Unhistorical Pastoral; A Romantic Farce; Bruce, a Chronicle Play; Smith, a Tragic Farce; Scaramouch in Naxos, a Pantomime. With a Frontispiece and Cover Design by AUBREY BEARDSLEY. Small 4to. 7s. 6d. net.

FLEET STREET ECLOGUES. Fcap. 8vo, buckram. 4s. 6d. net. [Third Edition.

FLEET STREET ECLOGUES. 2nd Series. Fcap. 8vo, buckram. 4s. 6d. net. [Second Edition.

A RANDOM ITINERARY AND A BALLAD. With a Frontispiece and Title-page by LAURENCE HOUSMAN. Fcap. 8vo, Irish Linen. 5s. net.

BALLADS AND SONGS. With a Title-page and Cover Design by WALTER WEST. Fcap. 8vo, buckram. 5s. net. [Fourth Edition.

NEW BALLADS. Fcap. 8vo, buckram. 4s. 6d. net.

## De Tabley (Lord)

POEMS, DRAMATIC AND LYRICAL. By JOHN LEICESTER WARREN (Lord de Tabley). Illustrations and Cover Design by C. S. RICKETTS. Crown 8vo. 7s. 6d. net. [Third Edition.

POEMS, DRAMATIC AND LYRICAL. Second Series, uniform in binding with the former volume. Crown 8vo. 5s. net.

## Duer (Caroline, and Alice).

POEMS. Fcap. 8vo. 3s. 6d. net.

## Egerton (George)

KEYNOTES. (See KEYNOTES SERIES.)

DISCORDS. (See KEYNOTES SERIES.)

YOUNG OFEG'S DITTIES. A translation from the Swedish of OLA HANSSON. With Title-page and Cover Design by AUBREY BEARDSLEY. Crown 8vo. 3s. 6d. net.

SYMPHONIES. [In preparation.

Eglinton (John).
TWO ESSAYS ON THE REMNANT.
Post 8vo, wrappers. 1s. 6d. net.
*Transferred to the present Pub-
lisher.* [*Second Edition.*

Eve's Library.
Each volume, crown 8vo. 3s. 6d.
net.
  I. MODERN WOMEN. An Eng-
     lish rendering of LAURA
     MARHOLM     HANSSON'S
     "DAS BUCH DER FRAUEN"
     by HERMIONE RAMSDEN.
     Subjects: Sonia Kovalevsky,
     George Egerton, Eleanora
     Duse, Amalie Skram, Marie
     Bashkirtseff, A. Ch. Edgren
     Lefiler.
  II. THE ASCENT OF WOMAN.
     By ROY DEVEREUX.
  III. MARRIAGE QUESTIONS IN
     MODERN FICTION. By
     ELIZABETH RACHEL CHAP-
     MAN.

Fea (Allan).
THE FLIGHT OF THE KING : a full,
true, and particular account of the
escape of His Most Sacred Ma-
jesty King Charles II. after the
Battle of Worcester, with Twelve
Portraits in Photogravure and
nearly 100 other Illustrations.
Demy 8vo. 21s. net.

Field (Eugene).
THE LOVE AFFAIRS OF A BIBLIO-
MANIAC. Post 8vo. 3s. 6d. net.

Fletcher (J. S.).
THE WONDERFUL WAPENTAKE.
By "A SON OF THE SOIL." With
18 full-page Illustrations by J. A.
SYMINGTON. Crown 8vo. 5s. 6d.
net.

LIFE IN ARCADIA. (*See* ARCADY
LIBRARY.)

GOD'S FAILURES. (*See* KEYNOTES
SERIES.)

BALLADS OF REVOLT. Sq. 32mo.
2s. 6d. net.

Ford (James L.).
THE LITERARY SHOP AND OTHER
TALES. Fcap. 8vo. 3s. 6d. net.

Four-and-Sixpenny Novels
Each volume with Title-page and
Cover Design by PATTEN WILSON.
Crown 8vo. 4s. 6d. net.
GALLOPING DICK. By H. B. MAR-
RIOTT WATSON.
THE WOOD OF THE BRAMBLES. By
FRANK MATHEW.
THE SACRIFICE OF FOOLS. By R.
MANIFOLD CRAIG.
A LAWYER'S WIFE. By Sir NEVILL
GEARY, Bart. [*Second Edition.*
*The following are in preparation :*
WEIGHED IN THE BALANCE. By
HARRY LANDER.
GLAMOUR. By META ORRED.
PATIENCE SPARHAWK AND HER
TIMES. By GERTRUDE ATHER-
TON.
THE WISE AND THE WAYWARD.
By G. S. STREET.
MIDDLE GREYNESS. By A. J. DAW-
SON.
THE MARTYR'S BIBLE. By GEORGE
FIFTH.
A CELIBATE'S WIFE. By HERBERT
FLOWERDEW.
MAX. By JULIAN CROSKEY.

Fuller (H. B.).
THE PUPPET BOOTH. Twelve Plays.
Crown 8vo. 4s. 6d. net.

Gale (Norman).
ORCHARD SONGS. With Title-page
and Cover Design by J. ILLING-
WORTH KAY. Fcap. 8vo, Irish
Linen. 5s. net.
Also a Special Edition limited in number
on hand-made paper bound in English
vellum. £1 1s. net.

Garnett (Richard).
POEMS. With Title-page by J.
ILLINGWORTH KAY. Crown 8vo.
5s. net.
DANTE, PETRARCH, CAMOENS,
cxxiv Sonnets, rendered in Eng-
lish. With Title-page by PATTEN
WILSON. Crown 8vo. 5s. net.

Gibson (Charles Dana).
PICTURES : Eighty-Five Large Car-
toons. Oblong Folio. 15s. net.
PICTURES OF PEOPLE. Eighty-Five
Large Cartoons. Oblong folio.
15s. net.
[*In preparation.*

## Gosse (Edmund).

THE LETTERS OF THOMAS LOVELL BEDDOES. Now first edited. Pott 8vo. 5s. net.

Also 25 copies large paper. 12s. 6d. net.

## Grahame (Kenneth).

PAGAN PAPERS. With Title-page by AUBREY BEARDSLEY. Fcap. 8vo. 5s. net.

[Out of Print at present.

THE GOLDEN AGE. With · Cover Design by CHARLES ROBINSON. Crown 8vo. 3s. 6d. net.

[Fifth Edition.

## Greene (G. A.).

ITALIAN LYRISTS OF TO-DAY. Translations in the original metres from about thirty-five living Italian poets, with bibliographical and biographical notes. Crown 8vo. 5s. net.

## Greenwood (Frederick).

IMAGINATION IN DREAMS. Crown 8vo. 5s. net.

## Hake (T. Gordon).

A SELECTION FROM HIS POEMS. Edited by Mrs. MEYNELL. With a Portrait after D. G. ROSSETTI, and a Cover Design by GLEESON WHITE. Crown 8vo. 5s. net.

## Hayes (Alfred).

THE VALE OF ARDEN AND OTHER POEMS. With a Title-page and a Cover designed by E. H. NEW. Fcap. 8vo. 3s. 6d. net.

Also 25 copies large paper. 15s. net.

## Hazlitt (William).

LIBER AMORIS; OR,. THE NEW PYGMALION. Edited, with an Introduction, by RICHARD LE GALLIENNE. To which is added an exact transcript of the original MS., Mrs. Hazlitt's Diary in Scotland, and letters never before published. Portrait after BE-WICK, and facsimile letters. 400 Copies only. 4to, 364 pp., buck-ram. 21s. net.

## Heinemann (William).

THE FIRST STEP; A Dramatic Moment. Small 4to. 3s. 6d. net.

## Hopper (Nora).

BALLADS IN PROSE. With a Title-page and Cover by WALTER WEST. Sq. 16mo. 5s. net.

UNDER QUICKEN BOUGHS. With Title-page designed by PATTEN WILSON, and Cover designed by ELIZABETH NAYLOR. Crown 8vo. 5s. net.

## Housman (Clemence).

THE WERE WOLF. With 6 full-page Illustrations, Title-page, and Cover Design by LAURENCE HOUSMAN. Sq. 16mo. 3s. 6d. net.

## Housman (Laurence).

GREEN ARRAS: Poems. With 6 Illustrations, Title-page, Cover Design, and End Papers by the Author. Crown 8vo. 5s. net.

GODS AND THEIR MAKERS. Crown 8vo, 5s. net. [In preparation.

## Irving (Laurence).

GODEFROI AND YOLANDE: A Play. Sm. 4to. 3s. 6d. net.

[In preparation.

## James (W. P.)

ROMANTIC PROFESSIONS: A Volume of Essays. With Title-page designed by J. ILLINGWORTH KAY. Crown 8vo. 5s. net.

## Johnson (Lionel).

THE ART OF THOMAS HARDY: Six Essays. With Etched Portrait by WM. STRANG, and Bibliography by JOHN LANE. Crown 8vo. 5s. 6d. net. [Second Edition.

Also 150 copies, large paper, with proofs of the portrait. £1 1s. net.

## Johnson (Pauline).

WHITE WAMPUM: Poems. With a Title-page and Cover Design by E. H. NEW. Crown 8vo. 5s. net.

## Johnstone (C. E.).

BALLADS OF BOY AND BEAK. With a Title-page by F. H. TOWNSEND. Sq. 32mo. 2s. net.

## Keynotes Series.

Each volume with specially-designed Title-page by AUBREY BEARDS-LEY or PATTEN WILSON. Crown 8vo, cloth. 3s. 6d. net.

I. KEYNOTES. By GEORGE EGERTON.
[*Seventh Edition.*

II. THE DANCING FAUN. By FLORENCE FARR.

III. POOR FOLK. Translated from the Russian of F. Dostoievsky by LENA MILMAN. With a Preface by GEORGE MOORE.

IV. A CHILD OF THE AGE. By FRANCIS ADAMS.

V. THE GREAT GOD PAN AND THE INMOST LIGHT. By ARTHUR MACHEN.
[*Second Edition.*

VI. DISCORDS. By GEORGE EGERTON.
[*Fifth Edition.*

VII. PRINCE ZALESKI. By M. P. SHIEL.

VIII. THE WOMAN WHO DID. By GRANT ALLEN.
[*Twenty-second Edition.*

IX. WOMEN'S TRAGEDIES. By H. D. LOWRY.

X. GREY ROSES. By HENRY HARLAND.

XI. AT THE FIRST CORNER AND OTHER STORIES. By H. B. MARRIOTT WATSON.

XII. MONOCHROMES. By ELLA D'ARCY.

XIII. AT THE RELTON ARMS. By EVELYN SHARP.

XIV. THE GIRL FROM THE FARM. By GERTRUDE DIX.
[*Second Edition.*

XV. THE MIRROR OF MUSIC. By STANLEY V. MAKOWER.

XVI. YELLOW AND WHITE. By W. CARLTON DAWE.

XVII. THE MOUNTAIN LOVERS. By FIONA MACLEOD.

XIII. THE WOMAN WHO DIDN'T. By VICTORIA CROSSE.
[*Third Edition.*

## Keynotes Series—*continued.*

XIX. THE THREE IMPOSTORS. By ARTHUR MACHEN.

XX. NOBODY'S FAULT. By NETTA SYRETT.
[*Second Edition.*

XXI. THE BRITISH BARBARIANS. By GRANT ALLEN.
[*Second Edition.*

XXII. IN HOMESPUN. By E. NESBIT.

XXIII. PLATONIC AFFECTIONS. By JOHN SMITH.

XXIV. NETS FOR THE WIND. By UNA TAYLOR.

XXV. WHERE THE ATLANTIC MEETS THE LAND. By CALDWELL LIPSETT.

XXVI. IN SCARLET AND GREY. By FLORENCE HENNIKER. (With THE SPECTRE OF THE REAL by FLORENCE HENNIKER and THOMAS HARDY.) [*Second Edition.*

XXVII. MARIS STELLA. By MARIE CLOTHILDE BALFOUR.

XXVIII. DAY BOOKS. By MABEL E. WOTTON.

XXIX. SHAPES IN THE FIRE. By M. P. SHIEL.

XXX. UGLY IDOL. By CLAUD NICHOLSON.

*The following are in rapid preparation:*

XXXI. KAKEMONOS. By W. CARLTON DAWE.

XXXII. GOD'S FAILURES. By J. S. FLETCHER.

XXXIII. A DELIVERANCE. By ALLAN MONKHOUSE.

XXXIV. MERE SENTIMENT. By A. J. DAWSON.

## Lane's Library.

Each volume crown 8vo. 3s. 6d. net.

I. MARCH HARES. By GEORGE FORTH.
[*Second Edition.*

II. THE SENTIMENTAL SEX. By GERTRUDE WARDEN.

III. GOLD. By ANNIE LINDEN.

## Lane's Library—*continued*.

*The following are in preparation:*
- IV. BROKEN AWAY. By BEATRICE GRIMSHAW.
- V. RICHARD LARCH. By E. A. BENNETT.
- VI. THE DUKE OF LINDEN. By JOSEPH F. CHARLES.

## Leather (R. K.).

VERSES. 250 copies. Fcap. 8vo. 3s. net. [*Transferred to the present Publisher.*

## Lefroy (Edward Cracroft.)

POEMS. With a Memoir by W. A. GILL, and a reprint of Mr. J. A. SYMONDS' Critical Essay on "Echoes from Theocritus." Cr. 8vo. Photogravure Portrait. 5s. net.

## Le Gallienne (Richard).

PROSE FANCIES. With Portrait of the Author by WILSON STEER. Crown 8vo. Purple cloth. 5s. net. [*Fourth Edition.*
Also a limited large paper edition. 12s. 6d. net.

THE BOOK BILLS OF NARCISSUS, An Account rendered by RICHARD LE GALLIENNE. With a Frontispiece. Crown 8vo, purple cloth. 3s. 6d. net. [*Third Edition.*
Also 50 copies on large paper. 8vo. 10s. 6d. net.

ROBERT LOUIS STEVENSON, AN ELEGY, AND OTHER POEMS, MAINLY PERSONAL. With Etched Title-page by D. Y. CAMERON. Crown 8vo, purple cloth. 4s. 6d. net.
Also 75 copies on large paper. 8vo. 12s. 6d. net.

ENGLISH POEMS. Crown 8vo, purple cloth. 4s. 6d. net. [*Fourth Edition, revised.*

GEORGE MEREDITH: Some Characteristics. With a Bibliography (much enlarged) by JOHN LANE, portrait, &c. Crown 8vo, purple cloth. 5s. 6d. net. [*Fourth Edition.*

## Le Gallienne (Richard)—*continued*.

THE RELIGION OF A LITERARY MAN. Crown 8vo, purple cloth. 3s. 6d. net. [*Fifth Thousand.*
Also a special rubricated edition on hand-made paper. 8vo. 10s. 6d. net.

RETROSPECTIVE REVIEWS, A LITERARY LOG, 1891-1895. 2 vols. Crown 8vo, purple cloth. 9s. net.

PROSE FANCIES. (Second Series). Crown 8vo, Purple cloth. 5s. net.

THE QUEST OF THE GOLDEN GIRL. Crown 8vo. 5s. net. [*In preparation.*

*See also* HAZLITT, WALTON and COTTON.

## Lowry (H. D.).

MAKE BELIEVE. Illustrated by CHARLES ROBINSON. Crown 8vo, gilt edges or uncut. 5s. net.

WOMEN'S TRAGEDIES. (*See* KEYNOTES SERIES).

## Lucas (Winifred).

UNITS: Poems. Fcap. 8vo. 3s. 6d. net.

## Lynch (Hannah).

THE GREAT GALEOTO AND FOLLY OR SAINTLINESS. Two Plays, from the Spanish of JOSÉ ECHEGARAY, with an Introduction. Small 4to. 5s. 6d. net.

## Marzials (Theo.).

THE GALLERY OF PIGEONS AND OTHER POEMS. Post 8vo. 4s. 6d. net. [*Transferred to the present Publisher.*

## The Mayfair Set.

Each volume fcap. 8vo. 3s. 6d. net.
- I. THE AUTOBIOGRAPHY OF A BOY. Passages selected by his friend G. S. STREET. With a Title-page designed by C. W. FURSE. [*Fifth Edition.*
- II. THE JONESES AND THE ASTERISKS. A Story in Monologue. By GERALD CAMPBELL. With a Title-page and 6 Illustrations by F. H. TOWNSEND. [*Second Edition.*

## The Mayfair Set—*continued.*

III. SELECT CONVERSATIONS WITH AN UNCLE, NOW EXTINCT. By H. G. WELLS. With a Title-page by F. H. TOWNSEND.

IV. FOR PLAIN WOMEN ONLY. By GEORGE FLEMING. With a Title-page by PATTEN WILSON.

V. THE FEASTS OF AUTOLYCUS: THE DIARY OF A GREEDY WOMAN. Edited by ELIZABETH ROBINS PENNELL. With a Title-page by PATTEN WILSON.

VI. MRS. ALBERT GRUNDY: OBSERVATIONS IN PHILISTIA. By HAROLD FREDERIC. With a Title-page by PATTEN WILSON.
*[Second Edition.*

## Meredith (George).

THE FIRST PUBLISHED PORTRAIT OF THIS AUTHOR, engraved on the wood by W. BISCOMBE GARDNER, after the painting by G. F. WATTS. Proof copies on Japanese vellum, signed by painter and engraver. £1 1s. net.

## Meynell (Mrs.).

POEMS. Fcap. 8vo. 3s. 6d. net.
*[Fourth Edition.*

THE RHYTHM OF LIFE AND OTHER ESSAYS. Fcap. 8vo. 3s. 6d. net.
*[Third Edition.*

THE COLOUR OF LIFE AND OTHER ESSAYS. Fcap 8vo. 3s. 6d. net. *[Second Edition.*

THE DARLING YOUNG. Fcap. 8vo. 3s. 6d. net. *[In preparation.*

## Miller (Joaquin).

THE BUILDING OF THE CITY BEAUTIFUL. Fcap. 8vo. With a Decorated Cover. 5s. net.

## Money-Coutts (F. B.).

POEMS. With Title-page designed by PATTEN WILSON. Crown 8vo. 3s. 6d. net.

## Monkhouse (Allan).

BOOKS AND PLAYS: A Volume of Essays on Meredith, Borrow, Ibsen, and others. Crown 8vo. 5s. net.

## Nesbit (E.).

A POMANDER OF VERSE. With a Title-page and Cover designed by LAURENCE HOUSMAN. Crown 8vo. 5s. net.

IN HOMESPUN. (*See* KEYNOTES SERIES.)

## Nettleship (J. T.).

ROBERT BROWNING: Essays and Thoughts. Crown 8vo. 5s. 6d. net. *[Third Edition.*

## Noble (Jas. Ashcroft).

THE SONNET IN ENGLAND AND OTHER ESSAYS. Title-page and Cover Design by AUSTIN YOUNG. Crown 8vo. 5s. net.

Also 50 copies large paper 12s. 6d. net

## Oppenheim (Michael).

A HISTORY OF THE ADMINISTRATION OF THE ROYAL NAVY, and of Merchant Shipping in relation to the Navy from MDIX to MDCLX, with an introduction treating of the earlier period. With Illustrations. Demy 8vo. 15s. net.

## O'Shaughnessy (Arthur).

HIS LIFE AND HIS WORK. With Selections from his Poems. By LOUISE CHANDLER MOULTON. Portrait and Cover Design. Fcap. 8vo. 5s. net.

## Oxford Characters.

A series of lithographed portraits by WILL ROTHENSTEIN, with text by F. YORK POWELL and others. 200 copies only, folio, buckram. £3 3s. net.

25 special large paper copies containing proof impressions of the portraits signed by the artist, £6 6s. net.

## Peters (Wm. Theodore).

POSIES OUT OF RINGS. With Title-page by PATTEN WILSON. Sq. 16mo. 2s. 6d. net.

## Pierrot's Library.

Each volume with Title-page, Cover and End Papers, designed by AUBREY BEARDSLEY. Sq. 16mo. 2s. net.

    I. PIERROT. By H. DE VERE STACPOOLE.
    II. MY LITTLE LADY ANNE. By Mrs. EGERTON CASTLE.
    III. SIMPLICITY. By A. T. G. PRICE.
    IV. MY BROTHER. By VINCENT BROWN.

*The following are in preparation:*

    V. DEATH, THE KNIGHT, AND THE LADY. By H. DE VERE STACPOOLE.
    VI. MR. PASSINGHAM. By THOMAS COBB.
    VII. TWO IN CAPTIVITY. By VINCENT BROWN.

## Plarr (Victor).

IN THE DORIAN MOOD: Poems. With Title-page by PATTEN WILSON. Crown 8vo. 5s. net.

## Radford (Dollie).

SONGS AND OTHER VERSES. With a Title-page by PATTEN WILSON. Fcap. 8vo. 4s. 6d. net.

## Rhys (Ernest).

A LONDON ROSE AND OTHER RHYMES. With Title-page designed by SELWYN IMAGE. Crown 8vo. 5s. net.

## Robertson (John M.).

ESSAYS TOWARDS A CRITICAL METHOD. (New Series.) Crown 8vo. 5s. net. [*In preparation.*

## St. Cyres (Lord).

THE LITTLE FLOWERS OF ST. FRANCIS: A new rendering into English of the Fioretti di San Francesco. Crown 8vo. 5s. net. [*In preparation.*

## Seaman (Owen).

THE BATTLE OF THE BAYS. Fcap. 8vo. 3s. 6d. net.

## Sedgwick (Jane Minot).

SONGS FROM THE GREEK. Fcap. 8vo. 3s. 6d. net.

## Setoun (Gabriel).

THE CHILD WORLD: Poems. Illustrated by CHARLES ROBINSON. Crown 8vo. gilt edges or uncut. 5s. net. [*In preparation.*

## Sharp (Evelyn).

WYMPS: Fairy Tales. With Coloured Illustrations by MABEL DEARMER. Small 4to, decorated cover. 4s. 6d. net. [*In preparation.*

AT THE RELTON ARMS. (*See* KEYNOTES SERIES.)

## Shore (Louisa).

POEMS. With an appreciation by FREDERIC HARRISON and a Portrait. Fcap. 8vo. 5s. net.

## Short Stories Series.

Each volume Post 8vo. Coloured edges. 2s. 6d. net.

    I. THE HINT O' HAIRST. By MÉNIE MURIEL DOWIE.
    II. THE SENTIMENTAL VIKINGS. By R. V. RISLEY.
    III. SHADOWS OF LIFE. By Mrs. MURRAY HICKSON.

## Stevenson (Robert Louis).

PRINCE OTTO. A Rendering in French by EGERTON CASTLE. With Frontispiece, Title-page, and Cover Design by D. Y. CAMERON. Crown 8vo. 7s. 6d. net.

Also 50 copies on large paper, uniform in size with the Edinburgh Edition of the Works.

A CHILD'S GARDEN OF VERSES. With over 150 Illustrations by CHARLES ROBINSON. Crown 8vo. 5s. net. [*Second Edition.*

## Stoddart (Thos. Tod).

THE DEATH WAKE. With an Introduction by ANDREW LANG. Fcap. 8vo. 5s. net.

## Street (G. S.).

EPISODES. Post 8vo. 3s. net.

MINIATURES AND MOODS. Fcap. 8vo. 3s. net. [*Both transferred to the present Publisher.*

QUALES EGO: A FEW REMARKS, IN PARTICULAR AND AT LARGE. Fcap. 8vo. 3s. 6d. net.

Street (G. S.)—*continued*.
THE AUTOBIOGRAPHY OF A BOY.
(*See* MAYFAIR SET.)
THE WISE AND THE WAYWARD.
(*See* FOUR - AND - SIXPENNY
NOVELS.)

Swettenham (F. A.)
MALAY SKETCHES. With a Title-
page and Cover Design by PATTEN
WILSON. Crown 8vo. 5s. net.
[*Second Edition*.

Tabb (John B.).
POEMS. Sq. 32mo. 4s. 6d. net.

Tennyson (Frederick).
POEMS OF THE DAY AND YEAR.
With a Title-page designed by
PATTEN WILSON. Crown 8vo.
5s. net.

Thimm (Carl A.).
A COMPLETE BIBLIOGRAPHY OF
FENCING AND DUELLING, AS
PRACTISED BY ALL EUROPEAN
NATIONS FROM THE MIDDLE
AGES TO THE PRESENT DAY.
With a Classified Index, arranged
Chronologically according to
Languages. Illustrated with
numerous Portraits of Ancient
and Modern Masters of the Art.
Title-pages and Frontispieces of
some of the earliest works. Por-
trait of the Author by WILSON
STEER, and Title-page designed
by PATTEN WILSON. 4to. 21s.
net.

Thompson (Francis).
POEMS. With Frontispiece, Title-
page, and Cover Design by
LAURENCE HOUSMAN. Pott 4to.
5s. net. [*Fourth Edition*.
SISTER-SONGS : An Offering to
Two Sisters. With Frontispiece,
Title-page, and Cover Design by
LAURENCE HOUSMAN. Pott 4to.
5s. net.

Thoreau (Henry David).
POEMS OF NATURE. Selected and
edited by HENRY S. SALT and
FRANK B. SANBORN, with a
Title-page designed by PATTEN
WILSON. Fcap. 8vo. 4s. 6d.
net.

Traill (H. D.).
THE BARBAROUS BRITISHERS : A
Tip-top Novel. With Title and
Cover Design by AUBREY
BEARDSLEY. Crown 8vo, wrap-
per. 1s. net.
FROM CAIRO TO THE SOUDAN
FRONTIER. With Cover Design
by PATTEN WILSON. Crown
8vo. 5s. net.

Tynan Hinkson (Katharine).
CUCKOO SONGS. With Title-page
and Cover Design by LAURENCE
HOUSMAN. Fcap. 8vo. 5s. net.
MIRACLE PLAYS. OUR LORD'S
COMING AND CHILDHOOD. With
6 Illustrations, Title-page, and
Cover Design by PATTEN WIL-
SON. Fcap. 8vo. 4s. 6d. net.

Walton and Cotton.
THE COMPLEAT ANGLER. Edited
by RICHARD LE GALLIENNE.
Illustrated by EDMUND H. NEW.
Crown 4to, decorated cover. 15s.
net.
Also to be had in twelve 1s. parts.

Watson (Rosamund Mar-
riott).
VESPERTILIA AND OTHER POEMS.
With a Title-page designed by R.
ANNING BELL. Fcap. 8vo. 4s. 6d.
net.
A SUMMER NIGHT AND OTHER
POEMS. New Edition. With a
Decorative Title-page. Fcap.
8vo. 3s. net.

Watson (William).
THE FATHER OF THE FOREST AND
OTHER POEMS. With New Photo-
gravure Portrait of the Author
Fcap. 8vo, buckram. 3s. 6d. net.
[*Fifth Edition*.
ODES AND OTHER POEMS. Fcap.
8vo, buckram. 4s. 6d. net.
[*Fourth Edition*.
THE ELOPING ANGELS : A Caprice
Square 16mo, buckram. 3s. 6d.
net. [*Second Edition*.
EXCURSIONS IN CRITICISM : being
some Prose Recreations of a
Rhymer. Crown 8vo, buckram.
5s. net. [*Second Edition*.

**Watson (William)**—*continued.*
THE PRINCE'S QUEST AND OTHER
POEMS. With a Bibliographical
Note added. Fcap. 8vo, buckram.
4s. 6d. net.    [*Third Edition.*
THE PURPLE EAST : A Series of
Sonnets on England's Desertion
of Armenia. With a Frontispiece
after G. F. WATTS, R.A. Fcap.
8vo, wrappers. 1s. net.
[*Third Edition.*

**Watt (Francis).**
THE LAW'S LUMBER ROOM. Fcap.
8vo. 3s. 6d. net.
[*Second Edition.*

**Watts-Dunton (Theodore).**
POEMS. Crown 8vo. 5s. net.
[*In preparation.*
There will also be an *Edition de Luxe* of
this volume printed at the Kelmscott
Press.

**Wharton (H. T.)**
SAPPHO. Memoir, Text, Selected
Renderings, and a Literal Trans-
lation by HENRY THORNTON
WHARTON. With 3 Illustra-
tions in Photogravure, and a
Cover designed by AUBREY
BEARDSLEY. Fcap. 8vo. 7s. 6d.
net.    [*Third Edition.*

---

# THE YELLOW BOOK

## An Illustrated Quarterly.

*Pott 4to.  5s. net.*

I. April 1894, 272 pp., 15 Illustrations.    [*Out of print.*

II. July 1894, 364 pp., 23 Illustrations.

III. October 1894, 280 pp., 15
Illustrations.

IV. January 1895, 285 pp., 16
Illustrations.

V. April 1895, 317 pp., 14 Illustrations.

VI. July 1895, 335 pp., 16 Illustrations.

VII. October 1895, 320 pp., 20
Illustrations.

VIII. January 1896, 406 pp., 26
Illustrations.

IX. April 1896, 256 pp., 17 Illustrations.

X. July 1896, 340 pp., 13 Illustrations.